SIR HOWARD THE COWARD

Sir Howard de Quincy Updike St. James has a fine name. But all who know him call him a coward.

"Sir Howard, the Coward," they say in dismay, "won't answer a challenge or fight with a dragon."

When the mighty Duke of Middlesex attacks, the young knight just has to do battle. He brings cookies to eat (in case he is caught) and puts on his armor completely unused.

'Though the fighting is fierce and the good men outnumbered, Sir Howard the Coward is a hero that day . . . or is he?

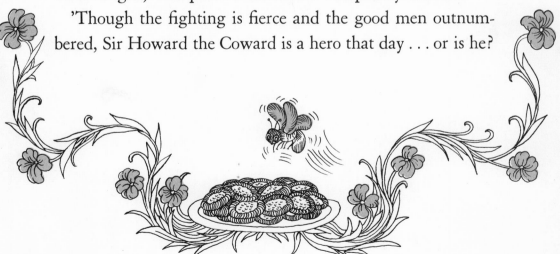

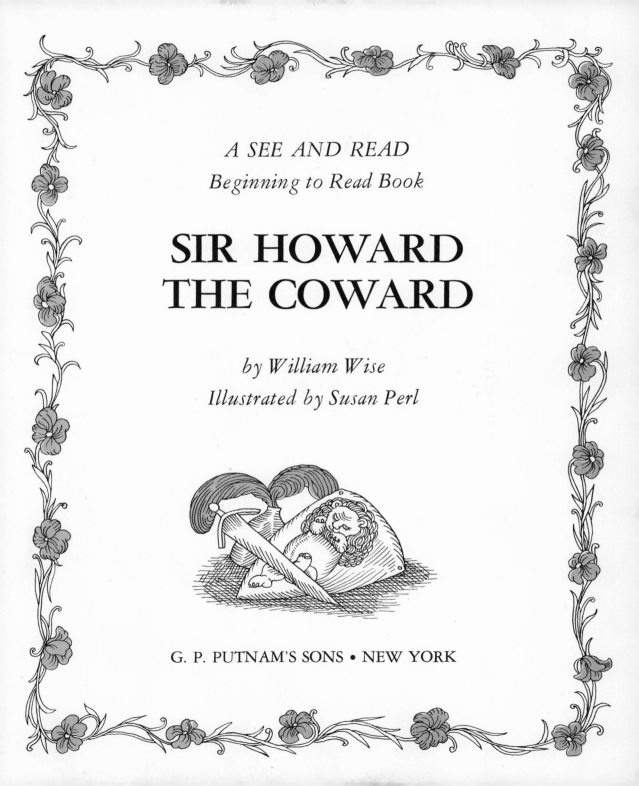

A SEE AND READ
Beginning to Read Book

SIR HOWARD
THE COWARD

by William Wise
Illustrated by Susan Perl

G. P. PUTNAM'S SONS • NEW YORK

Published simultaneously in the Dominion of
Canada by Longmans Canada Limited, Toronto
Library of Congress Catalog Card Number: 67-24182
PRINTED IN THE UNITED STATES OF AMERICA
06208

Once there was a young knight
who lived with his father and mother
in an old stone castle.
His name was Sir Howard de Quincy Updike St. James.
He had a fine sword.
He had a shield with a lion on it.
And he had a new and beautiful suit of silver armor.

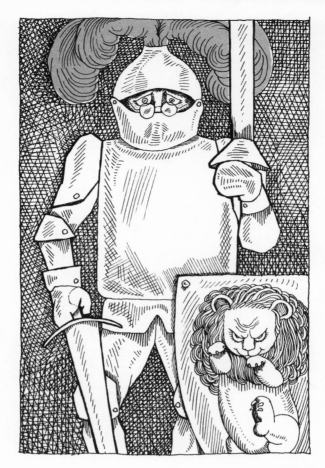

No other knight in all the kingdom
looked better than Sir Howard did,
when he was dressed for battle.
The only trouble was that
AFTER he was dressed for battle
he never seemed to do any fighting.

When another knight rode by and challenged him,
he made up excuses.
"My shield has a hole in it!" he would shout
from the top of the castle.
"My armor is too tight!
And I've just sent my sword out to be fixed!
But there's nothing like a good fight, I always say.
Please DO come back and challenge me another time!"

Sir Howard never saved anyone from a dragon either.

"If I get too near a dragon," he would say,

"I always get sick.

My nose begins to run.

My eyes begin to water.

A lot of big red spots come out all over me.

But I know you need help.

So let me send you down the road

to the knight who lives in the very next castle.

People say he's a wonder with dragons.

He'll take care of yours for you, in no time at all!"

In this way, a few years went by.
Sir Howard never answered the challenge
of another knight.
He never saved anyone from a dragon.
Little by little, people began to wonder why.
Could it be that he was AFRAID to fight?

People wondered, people watched, people waited.
But Sir Howard de Quincy Updike St. James
only made up more excuses.
At last everyone saw that he NEVER
was going to do any fighting.
And then, from one end of the kingdom to the other,
they began to call him 'Sir Howard, the Coward.'

Sir Howard's father, the old Earl of St. James,
grew very angry.
"How could a famous warrior like me
have a son like you?" he cried.
"Why, when I was a young knight,
fighting was all that I ever did!"

11

"But Father, you LIKED to fight,"
said Sir Howard,
"while I like to do other things.
I like to make cakes and cookies
in the castle kitchen.

12

I like to catch fish
in the castle moat.
And I like to work magic tricks
in the magic room."

"A knight should do nothing but fight!"
shouted the old Earl.
"He should save people from dragons!
When I was young, that's what I did,
and I became famous for it!"

Sir Howard's mother, the Countess of St. James,
did not grow angry. But she did grow very sad.
"If only you would fight just once,"
she said to Sir Howard,
"then everything would be all right."

"Do you think just once would be enough?"
asked Sir Howard.

"I KNOW it would!" said the Countess.

"Then I will fight the very next knight
who challenges me!" Sir Howard said.

"Unless my shield has a hole in it.

Or unless my armor is too tight.

Or unless . . ."

But the Countess was not listening any more.

Then one morning, a knight rode quickly
into the castle.
"Your lifelong enemy is coming to do battle!"
he shouted to the old Earl.
"The mighty Duke of Middlesex
and his Five-Famous-Warrior-Sons,
are coming at the head of a great army!"

"To arms! Once more to arms!" cried the old Earl.
"Call all my friends and neighbors to the castle!
Tell them that in an hour I will take the field
against the mighty Duke of Middlesex!
And say that my son, Sir Howard,
will ride with me into battle!"

But almost everyone was afraid
of the mighty Duke
and his Five-Famous-Warrior-Sons.
An hour later, only a few other knights
had come to help the old Earl.
And most of them were as old as he was.

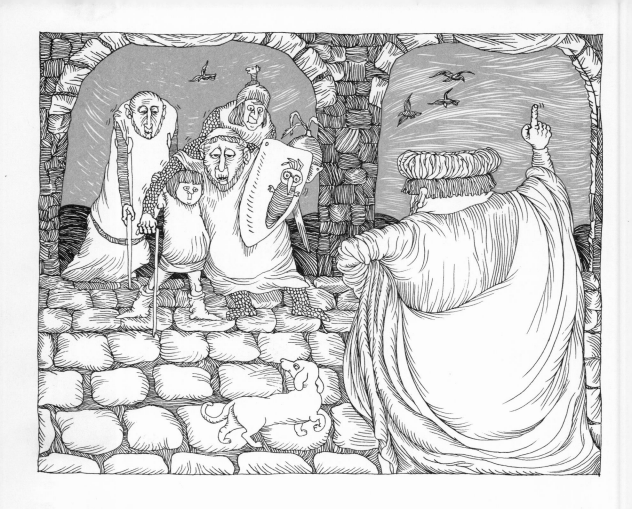

"Who cares?" said the old Earl.

"The fewer we are, the more famous we will be after winning the battle!

Now, where is Sir Howard?

Where is my son?"

Sir Howard was not to be seen.
They called out his name,
but no one answered.
The old Earl began to turn very red.
He ground his teeth together,
because he was so angry.
Then he ran back into the castle
to look for his son.

He looked in the armor room,
but Sir Howard was not there.
He looked in the kitchen,
but Sir Howard was not there either.
He looked in the music room ...
and in the magic room ...
and even under the castle in the deepest dungeon ...
but Sir Howard de Quincy Updike St. James
was not in any of them.

At last the old Earl
went to his son's bedroom.
He looked under the bed.
And that was where he found him.

Then the old Earl grew even more angry.
"The time has come to fight!" he said.
"What do you think you're doing
under that bed?"

"I was only looking
for my shield," said Sir Howard.
"Well, come out and take THIS shield!"
the old Earl shouted,
pulling one down from the wall.
"And get into your suit of armor!
We must fight the mighty Duke of Middlesex today —"

"TODAY?" cried Sir Howard.
"But I can't fight anyone TODAY!"
Why, my sword is still out being fixed!
And my armor is still too tight!
And —"

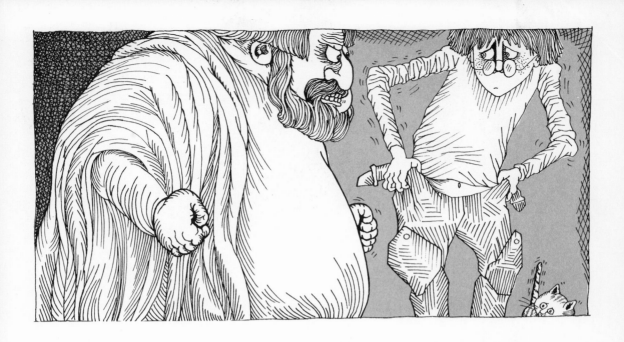

"Stop making up excuses!" shouted the old Earl.
"You have ten minutes
to get dressed for battle!
If you're not ready by then . . .!"
The sound of his teeth,
as he ground them together,
was really terrible.
Ten minutes later
Sir Howard was out of the castle,
and seated on his horse.

They all rode away from the castle
and they came to the top of a hill.
"The enemy will be here soon,"
the old Earl said.
"We must hide in the forest.
And when they ride by,
we will fall upon them from ambush!"

The old Earl, Sir Howard, and the others
hid in the forest.
Then they watched the mighty Duke,
and his great army, coming nearer.

It was a terrible thing to see.

At least Sir Howard thought it was terrible.

"The Duke has so many knights!"
he said to his father.

"Why, he must have
three or four times as many
as we have!"

"More like TWENTY times as many!"
said the old Earl.

"If they win the battle," said Sir Howard,
"they will take us prisoner.
And keep us in a dungeon all night long!"
"More like all YEAR long," said the old Earl.

"But he who turns and runs away,"
said Sir Howard,
"lives to fight another day!"

"He who tries THAT," said the old Earl,
"will be sorry when he meets up with ME!"

Sir Howard began to feel very hot.
He opened his helmet, to cool himself off.
"Dear me," he thought,
"how I wish I were back at the castle,
doing something else!"
Just then, the old Earl looked around.
"Why is your helmet open?" he asked.
"You can't ride into battle like that.
Here, you fool, I will shut it for you!"
But as the old Earl shut Sir Howard's helmet,
something surprising happened.

For Sir Howard had hidden some cakes and cookies
inside his armor
(just in case the Earl lost the battle).

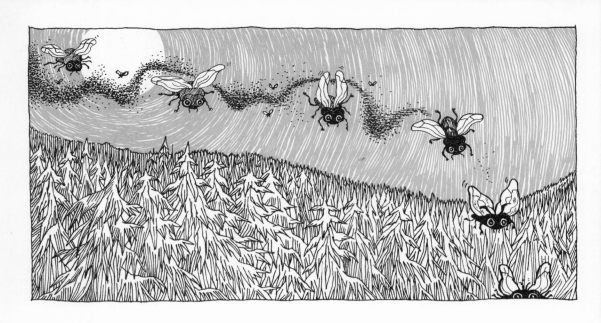

The cakes and cookies were very sweet.
No sooner had Sir Howard opened his helmet,
than some flies began
to smell how sweet they were.
So did a hornet.

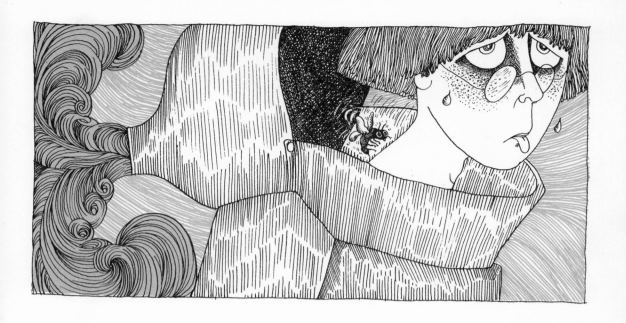

The hornet had just landed
on the back of Sir Howard's neck
when the old Earl shut his helmet.

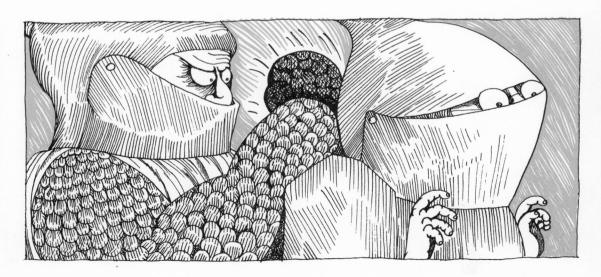

After a minute or two, Sir Howard said,
"Something is crawling around
inside this suit of armor!"
"Keep quiet!" said the old Earl,
"or you'll give away our ambush!"

"It must be a fly. I can hear it buzz.

Now it's started

to crawl down my back!"

"Keep quiet, I tell you!" said the old Earl.

"How can I keep quiet?" said Sir Howard.

"I must get it out!

I can't go into battle

with a fly buzzing around in here!

Now, if I could only put my hand down inside —"

All at once, a terrible cry rang out.
It was the most terrible cry
that ever had been heard in the kingdom.
It sounded like a great army of men
shouting together as loud as they could.

The next minute, a knight
in a beautiful suit of silver armor
flew out of the forest.
With a wave of his sword,
he rode down on the enemy.

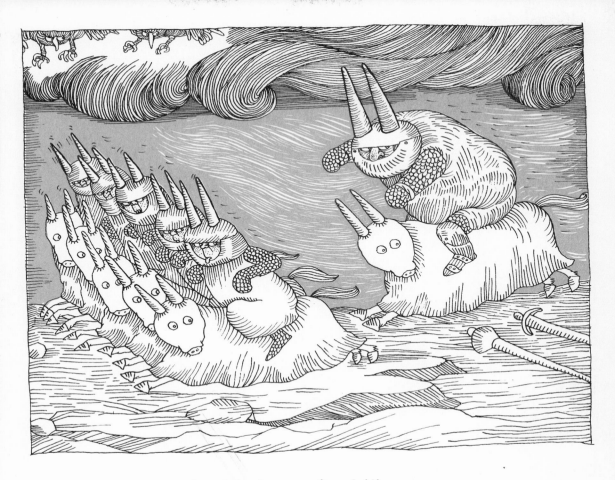

"An ambush! An ambush!"
cried the mighty Duke of Middlesex.
"There's an army hiding in the forest!"
cried his Five-Famous-Warrior-Sons.
And they all turned their horses,
and tried to ride away.

But Sir Howard, and the old Earl and the others
were too quick for them.
The old Earl and his friends
scattered many of the enemy.
But they did not scatter half as many
as the knight
in the beautiful suit of silver armor.

The battle was soon over.
The mighty Duke of Middlesex
and his Five-Famous-Warrior-Sons
were made prisoner.
Then the old Earl and his knights
went back to the castle.

The Countess saw the old Earl coming home.
She ran to meet him.
"Did Sir Howard
take any part in the battle?" she asked.
"Take ANY part?" cried the Earl.
"Why, he almost won the battle by himself!
Our son is the hero of the day!"

Everyone in the castle
began to shout Sir Howard's name,
over and over again.
At last, the shouting stopped.

Then Sir Howard said,
"Friends, knights, warriors —
do not call me a hero!
I really did nothing.
I was lucky, that's all.
I did not know what I was doing,
back there on the field of battle!"

The other knights laughed and laughed.
"He did nothing!
He was lucky!
He did not know what he was doing,
back there on the field of battle!"

When the laughing stopped,
Sir Howard tried to tell them
about the cakes and cookies
inside his armor.
And how a wild hornet flew in
and stung him.
"It kept on stinging me," he said,
"And *I* kept on waving my sword.
And that's how
I happened to scatter so many of the enemy."

But no one believed him.
Cakes and cookies? Wild stinging hornets?
How foolish!
He was now the most famous warrior
in the kingdom!
Sir Howard de Quincy Updike St. James —
Sir Howard, the Hero!

After that, life at the castle
was never the same.
The old Earl smiled,
and told people about his famous son.

The Countess smiled too,
because no one called him
"Sir Howard, the Coward" any more.

As for Sir Howard himself —
he smiled as much
as his father or mother did.
And that was because everyone knew
that he COULD fight —
so nobody ever asked him to do it again.

He did try to keep people
from making a fuss over him, though.
"Cakes and cookies won the battle,"
he always said.
"Cakes and cookies — and a wild, stinging hornet!"

But no one would listen.
From one end of the kingdom to the other
they said he was a hero.

And Sir Howard, the Hero he remained,
for the rest of his days.

Key Words

ambush	helmet
armor	hero
battle	Kingdom
castle	knight
challenge	moat
Countess	prisoner
dragon	shield
Duke	silver
dungeon	sting (ing), stung
Earl	sword
enemy	warrior
fuss	wild

About William Wise

WILLIAM WISE is the prize-winning author of more than a dozen books for young readers, including *In the Time of the Dinosaurs, The World of Giant Mammals,* and *The Two Reigns of Tutankhamen* which received a Boys' Clubs of America Junior Book Award Medal. Mr. Wise's *Alexander Hamilton,* a Junior Literary Guild Selection, has been reprinted extensively by the United States Information Service. It has appeared in special Asian and South American Editions, and has been translated into Portuguese and Bengali.

About Susan Perl

Readers will readily recognize the talented hand of Susan Perl in the drawings accompanying Sir Howard's misadventures. Miss Perl's delicately humorous art is familiar to readers of *The New York Times,* leading magazines, and many children's books. Miss Perl's contributions to the Putnam list include THE WONDERFUL WHISTLE, and THE BARBER OF SEVILLE, based on the Rossini opera and included among the children's books of 1966 recommended by the Child Study Association of America.